THE LOST WORLD

ELLIK THE LIGHTNING HORROR

With special thanks to Lucy Courtenay

For Will, with love

www.beastquest.co.uk

ORCHARD BOOKS
338 Euston Road, London NW1 3BH
Orchard Books Australia
Level 17/207 Kent St, Sydney, NSW 2000

A Paperback Original
First published in Great Britain in 2010

Beast Quest is a registered trademark of Working Partners Limited
Series created by Beast Quest Limited, London

A CIP catalogue record for this book is available from
the British Library.

ISBN 978 1 40830 733 5

9 10 8

Printed and bound by CPI Group (UK) Ltd, Croydon, CR0 4YY

The paper and board used in this paperback are natural recyclable
products made from wood grown in sustainable forests. The
manufacturing processes conform to the environmental regulations of
the country of origin.

Orchard Books is a division of Hachette Children's Books,
an Hachette UK company

www.hachette.co.uk

ELLIK
THE LIGHTNING HORROR

BY ADAM BLADE

THE FOREST OF DOOM
SOUTHERN RIVER
THE SCARLET DESERT

Tavania
THE FROZEN FIELDS
THE PLAINS
THE KING'S PALACE
THE MISTY JUNGLE

Welcome to another world, where Dark Forces are at play.

Tom thought he was on his way back home; he was wrong. My son has entered another realm where nothing is as it seems. Six monstrous Beasts threaten all corners of the kingdom, and Tom and Elenna must face an enemy they thought long gone. I have never been so proud of my son, but can he be all that I always hoped he would be? Or shall a mother watch her son fail?

One question remains. Are you brave enough to join Tom on the most deadly Quest yet?

Only you know the answer...

Freya, Mistress of the Beasts

PROLOGUE

Barbo the monkey sat high up in the branches of the Misty Jungle, swinging her furry brown tail.

She lifted her nose and sniffed, smelling ripe fruit nearby. Chattering softly to herself, she slipped off her branch and hung upside-down by her tail. She spotted the fruit on a neighbouring tree. She reached out and plucked a round, ripe papaya.

Still hanging upside down, she bit into it and sucked hungrily at the juice.

On other branches, the rest of the monkey troop was also feeding.

Barbo finished her papaya and dropped the skin. She pulled herself the right way round. A star fruit twinkled temptingly, just out of reach. She sprang across two branches and pulled the succulent fruit from its nest of leaves.

As she was eating, Barbo saw her sister, Chiro, swinging towards her. The two monkeys greeted each other, grunting affectionately. Chiro began to comb through Barbo's fur, hunting for fleas. Feeling full and contented, Barbo settled down on a wide branch and started to doze - when a fizzing, crackling sound down on the jungle floor made her eyes snap open.

The other monkeys shrieked in alarm, racing nimbly along the branches with their tails streaking behind them. Through the canopy of leaves, Barbo saw dark clouds roll across the sky. Sheet lightning flashed against the clouds, bathing the Misty Jungle in light. Chiro shook the branch with her feet, opening her mouth and showing her yellow teeth. Barbo's hackles rose. Trouble!

The troop ran swiftly to the tops of the trees to check the source of the danger. Barbo followed as best she could, stretching her arms to reach the branches and pull herself upwards.

More lightning forked through the sky, white and deadly. This time it was closer. Barbo was confused. Rain usually followed lightning, but no rain was falling.

Fruit fell to the ground as the monkeys abandoned their banquet. Their alarm calls rippled up and down the jungle. Barbo felt Chiro beside her, pushing her along. She was terrified, but forced her trembling limbs to move.

The lightning struck once again, splitting a nearby trunk in two with a crack and a burst of flame. Half-blinded by the brilliant light, Barbo thought she saw a huge shadow moving somewhere below the forest canopy. But the smell of burning filled her nostrils and she shrieked in panic. Where was Chiro? Barbo called desperately, but her cries were lost amid all the noise. Putting on a frantic burst of speed, Barbo streaked along a branch. She didn't dare look back. Something big was chasing them. The other monkeys were blurs, vaulting between the trees.

Barbo saw a great gap between the trees up ahead. She knew at once it was too wide for her to jump. The other monkeys were bolting at full speed, leaping through the air and scrabbling for footholds on the tips of the trees beyond. Several tumbled, spiralling through the air and crashing into the leaves below.

Barbo reached the last branch. She flung herself desperately into the air, stretching every sinew…

Something hit her soundlessly from behind. Everything went white. Barbo's fur stood on end, and she could smell that it was burning. She lost the feeling in her limbs, and tumbled past the safety of the outstretched branches.

She rolled over and over, head over heels, snatching with her tail and paws for something to slow her fall.

Barbo landed in a heap at the bottom of a tree, the wind knocked out of her. The other monkeys' howls were disappearing into the distance.

She was alone.

A shadow fell over Barbo's head. The young monkey went rigid with terror as she gazed at the scaly creature before her. It was as long and thick as a tree, with fins on its back that shimmered with rainbow colours. Its head was blunt and smooth, and reminded Barbo of a snake. A giant snake! A long forked tongue flickered between its lips, as if it could taste Barbo's fear.

Lightning struck again. It seemed to hit the Beast, which swayed and

lurched at the blow. But rather than being harmed, a pulsing blue glow spread over the Beast's scales. Its blood-red eyes swivelled and latched onto Barbo. They shone hungrily. The Beast reared up, opening its terrible mouth to reveal a set of long fangs.

As it darted forward, Barbo knew it was all over.

CHAPTER ONE

ACCUSATIONS

Tom stared at the row of angry faces as Malvel's soldier, Nathan, knelt down beside the injured boy. The young cattle thief was moaning with his eyes closed. His face was grey, and his back was cut to ribbons, his skin torn apart by the fangs and claws of Madara, the Midnight Warrior. Blood stained the ground among the rocks.

"Do you think he'll survive?" Elenna said, but Nathan gave her a cold stare. Her wolf Silver pressed against her, and she stroked his shaggy coat. "Madara was so strong," she continued. "He didn't stand a chance."

"You lie!" said Nathan. "You two did this. Get your hands up!"

Tom raised his arms. He wished they had defeated Madara the Midnight Warrior before she harmed the boy. The black portal in the sky had closed as soon as Tom had sent Madara back to the place he had come from. Now the sky above them was glassy and still again. There was no way to prove to the soldiers what had really happened.

Tom was tired of this land. Tavania was so similar to Avantia, their homeland, even though it looked the same, in many ways it was not. Here places had different names, and everything was hostile. Malvel was on the throne instead of the Good King Hugo. And Tom and Elenna weren't only fighting the Evil Wizard and angry Beasts; it was as if the land itself was against them.

There was a sudden commotion behind them. Tom whirled around, making his stallion, Storm, start. His hand went to his sword, before he remembered it had already been taken from him.

"Keep your hands up!" shouted Nathan.

An older man thrust himself through to the front. His grizzled face filled with horror as he stared at the boy on the ground. Tom recognised him at once from the day before, when they'd disguised themselves among the soldiers on their search for Madara.

"What have you done to my son?" said the man.

A murmur spread among the soldiers. They could not have known the boy's father was among them. Tom heard more swords being drawn and someone to the rear shouted, "We should punish them now!"

"We didn't—" Elenna began.

A groan from the boy interrupted her. Blood was seeping from the terrible gashes inflicted by Madara's wicked claws.

The old soldier, his father, knelt beside him and reached out his hand. "Jude," he said. "Speak to me, boy. What have these young villains done to you?"

The boy writhed in pain, and the old soldier looked up at Tom. His eyes passed over Tom's bloody hands and clothing. Anger flooded his face.

"It wasn't us," Tom said steadily.

"We would never do this!" Elenna protested.

"Lies!" The threat in the old soldier's voice was unmistakable. "Nothing but lies." He jumped to his feet. His sword flashed from its sheath as he levelled it at Tom. "I should kill you now," he said.

Tom kept as still as he could. The blade wobbled a hair's breadth from his neck. The old man's eyes were glassy with tears.

"No, Erco," warned Nathan. "These are the two that King Malvel wants alive. We'll get a reward if we take them back to the castle."

Erco didn't seem to hear. He tightened his grip on his sword, pressing the tip to Tom's throat. Tom felt a nick of pain and the warm trickle of blood on his neck.

"Erco," said Nathan desperately. "We can't disobey the king. It's not worth it."

Erco's jaw hardened and he lowered

his sword. Tom recognised the look of fear in the old soldier's face.

"Tie them up," Nathan ordered his men.

Silver growled and bared his teeth as the soldiers came forward with ropes. One of the men raised his sword, ready to slash at the wolf.

"No!" Elenna shouted in horror. "It's all right, Silver. Everything's fine. Stay there."

Silver dropped back, growling but obedient. Tom and Elenna's weapons – the sword, shield and spear they'd stolen earlier – were taken away by Peter, one of the junior guards.

They were herded towards another open-backed cart at sword-point. The soldiers wrapped coarse ropes around their ankles and wrists and pushed them back onto the straw.

Tom didn't struggle: there'd be a time and place to make their escape. As two more soldiers cautiously bound Silver's jaws and tied him to the cart, Storm was led to the front, snorting and skittering sideways.

Erco laid his son on the straw beside Tom. The boy's eyes fluttered open. "Not them..." he mumbled. "Giant...white cat..."

"Hush, Jude," said Erco. "Just rest. You don't know what you're saying."

There was a shout from the front of the cart. Storm was rearing and lashing out with his hooves.

Tom struggled up on to his bound elbows. "Storm!" he called. "It will be all right. Trust me!"

Storm calmed down at the sound of Tom's voice, and let the soldiers harness him to the poles.

Tom heard a whip slice through the air and crack against Storm's skin. The stallion whinnied in pain.

"Hey!" Tom shouted. "Stop that!"

"You're in no position to be giving orders," sneered the soldier driving the cart. He cracked the whip again and the cart jolted forward. Silver ran beside the wheel, ropes trailing from his bound jaws. His eyes were fixed on Tom and Elenna.

"Poor Silver," Elenna said. "Those ropes are too tight."

As the cart rumbled along, Tom sank back against the straw and closed his eyes. Soon he and his companions would be presented to Malvel as trophies.

My Quest will have failed, he thought. *Despite everything we've been through, Malvel will have won.*

CHAPTER TWO

UNDER GUARD

"We can't let ourselves be taken back to Malvel," whispered Elenna.

Tom peered through the slats of the cart as it jolted down the road. Their cart was at the back of a convoy made up of five or six.

The weapons are in the second cart," said Tom. "We'll escape as soon as we get a chance and raid it."

But Tom knew he didn't even have a plan. As the cart rolled over a hole in the road, he was thrown from side to side. Unable to move his hands to stop himself rolling around, he felt bruised and battered all over. One look at Elenna's face told him she was feeling the same. Silver padded along behind them, whining softly.

The convoy trundled on through the hottest part of the day and Tom watched the sun rise through the sky and begin to dip once more. From this he could tell they were heading towards Malvel's castle. Erco came on board every so often to offer his injured son water from a flask, but the boy barely opened his eyes.

"Let me examine him," Elenna offered. "I might be able to help."

Erco rounded on her. "A likely story," the soldier sneered. "I'm not going to fall for your tricks again."

Tom knew it wasn't worth trying to reason with Erco. He only hoped that Jude recovered before they reached the castle. Then the truth would be known. As dusk drew over the sky, Nathan's voice called out to stop.

"Where are we?" Elenna asked as they lurched to a halt.

Tom raised himself up as best he could and peered over the side of the cart. On the horizon, he could just make out the towers of Malvel's castle, standing like a dark silhouette. The front three carts had stopped a short way ahead, and were drawn around in a circle. The soldiers were busy stretching their legs and putting up tents. The jolting and bumping eased as the wheels on Tom and Elenna's cart slowed and stopped. Storm whinnied and stamped his hooves.

"Looks like we're stopping here for the night," Tom said.

No one came to loosen their bonds, and soldiers were ordered off to fetch firewood. Tom shivered beside Elenna, and poor Jude mumbled words Tom couldn't hear. The stars glittered above, and the air was soon filled with the crackle of a campfire and the tempting smells of roasting meat. A single guard stayed beside Tom and Elenna's cart, his armour glinting in the firelight.

Tom's throat was dry and his stomach growled with hunger.

"The smell of that food is torture," Elenna said.

Tom could hear the soldiers laughing and joking. Only Erco seemed unwilling to join in.

"Malvel will be pleased we captured

these ruffians," came Nathan's voice. "You did well not to kill them, Erco. We'll probably get a ransom."

"Don't be too confident, Nathan," said another. "We haven't delivered them yet. Malvel's rage will be terrible if we fail."

The jokes and laughter faded away.

The soldiers finished their meal in sullen silence. Before long, the air was filled with their snores, and the light from the fire began to die. Tom strained at the ropes, but they cut into his wrists. He gritted his teeth against the pain.

"Hey, you!" Tom called to Peter, the young soldier guarding them. He shifted into an upright position as best he could. "Bring us food and water, for pity's sake!"

"Not a chance," Peter said with a nasty smile. Tom sank back, but started up again at the sound of the young cattle thief's voice beside him.

"I'm sorry you were caught," Jude whispered. "It's my fault. I tried to tell my father, but who would understand..."

His voice faltered. Tom guessed he

was thinking of the Beast.

"I know what you saw," said Tom, "but the others won't believe it. We're here to put the Beasts of Tavania back in their rightful homes, so they won't hurt anyone again. You have to help us."

The cattle thief's eyes opened wider. He looked at Tom uneasily. "But my father will be in trouble with the King. You heard him..."

"Malvel is the cause of Tavania's troubles," said Elenna. "The guard will fetch food and water if you ask, and you can set us free. Then we can continue our Quest to free Tavania."

"But how are you going to stop Malvel?" Jude protested. "Everyone's afraid of him. Even the soldiers."

"Just release us," said Elenna, "and we'll do the rest."

Tom leant closer to Jude's ear. "We aren't alone," he said. "When you reach the castle, find the warrior, Freya. She holds the key to Tavania's destiny. Freya is training a new hero to help battle Malvel."

"I know Malvel is a bad king," Jude said. "And I know other people think the same. Very well. I'll do it."

Tom's heart pounded as Jude rolled upright, wincing.

"Hey, Peter," he called. "Fetch water, will you? And food? I'm feeling stronger, but I'm so hungry I could eat the straw I'm lying on."

"I cannot leave my post," said Peter, eyeing Tom and Elenna.

"They aren't going anywhere," said Jude. "They're tied up, remember?"

Peter nodded stiffly. With a last suspicious glance at Tom and Elenna, he walked away.

As soon as Peter was out of sight, Jude fumbled with the ropes. Tom felt them loosen, then pulled his hands free. He went to work on Elenna's bonds straight away.

"Thank you," he said to Jude. "You've done a brave thing."

"We need weapons," said Elenna, quickly untying her feet.

"Peter won't be long," Jude warned.

Tom kicked away the last rope that bound his feet. He slipped off the back of the cart and crouched low to the ground, keeping guard as Elenna crept across and untied Silver. Then he slid on his belly towards the cart containing the weapons.

The light from the glowing embers cast shadows on the faces of the sleeping soldiers. Erco sat back, his mouth open and his eyes closed. Nathan lay sprawled on his front. Tom could see the shadowy figure of Peter, scooping water from a barrel on the far side of the camp.

The back of the weapons cart was unlatched. Tom eased it down and felt around in the darkness. His hand closed on a crossbow and a quiver of

bolts. They'd be perfect for Elenna. He reached again, retrieving a sword and shield for himself.

The quiver knocked against a pile of swords stacked in the cart. Tom froze. Nathan grunted, flung his arm up and turned over. Tom glimpsed Peter's head snapping around, warily. It seemed like an eternity before he bent to the water barrel again.

He crept back to find Elenna loosening the ropes that tied Storm to the cart. His horse nuzzled him, silently grateful. Tom tossed the quiver and crossbow at Elenna and hoisted himself onto Storm's back. Elenna climbed up behind him. As the stallion trotted softly away, Tom caught Jude's voice.

"Good luck!" the cattle thief called softly. "Tavania goes with you!"

CHAPTER THREE

STAMPEDE!

When they were at a safe distance, Tom nudged Storm into a gallop. He hoped Jude would use all his cattle-thief cunning to prevent Peter from discovering their escape until the morning.

The moon cast long grey shadows on the stony ground. Once the flames from the campfires had disappeared, Tom drew Storm to a halt, took the golden map from his saddlebags and unfolded it. Down on the ground, Silver moved to a trickling stream that snaked beside the track, and drank deeply.

Tom angled the map towards the moon to catch its gleam, and read the patterns etched into the patchwork of golden metal. His gaze fell on the castle marked in the centre of the map. Looking up, Tom saw the castle looming ahead, crouched on its rocky outcropping like a giant crow. But it was the south-western corner that drew Tom's eyes.

"A portal," Elenna said, looking over his shoulder.

The map showed a forested area called the Misty Jungle – in exactly the same place as the Dark Jungle back in Avantia. Shimmering above the jungle was a jagged black cloud that pulsed and moved beneath Tom's fingers.

"That's where we'll find the next Beast," he said.

A name was engraved in tiny, elegant letters above the portal. Ellik.

"What kind of Beast will Ellik be, do you think?" Elenna asked.

"I don't know," Tom admitted. He folded the map and replaced it in the saddlebag. "But whatever it is, it'll be angry. No one likes being taken from their home and thrown into a strange land. We have to send it back before it can cause too much damage."

They pressed on as the sky began to lighten. Weird colours shot through the air as the sun struggled to penetrate the glassy surface of the sky. Tom felt a surge of sadness as he guided Storm along rough paths, keeping a look out for any scouting parties that might be on the road leading towards the castle gates. Back in Avantia, King Hugo's castle was a symbol of justice, loyalty and trust. But here in the twisted kingdom of Tavania, it was an evil place.

Suddenly, the sky seemed to split apart as a flash of white lightning tore through the clouds.

Tom and Elenna shaded their eyes from the glare.

"It's coming from the south," said Elenna. "The same direction as the Misty Jungle."

"We'll follow the lightning," Tom said.

The ground began to rise steeply, and jagged mountain edges emerged in the dawn light. They struggled up small, narrow tracks that seemed to double back on themselves. Soon Storm's legs were trembling with exhaustion.

"We're not getting any closer to the lightning or the jungle," Elenna said in frustration, as they faced yet another hairpin bend. "Are we even still going in the right direction?"

Tom stretched his aching back and patted Storm's sweat-soaked neck.

"We have to go on," he said.

His friend gave a cry of relief when at last, the rocky cliffs melted away and they could see what lay beyond the mountains. The horizon was thick with the bright bottle-green foliage of the Misty Jungle. Sheet lightning was rippling from the sky directly above the trees. It was like no storm Tom had ever seen.

Elenna clung on tight as Tom dug his heels into Storm's flanks. The stallion leaped forwards, his strong legs powering down the track towards the jungle with Silver streaking alongside.

As the sun rose higher, the heat seemed to press down on them, and the air was thick with moisture. They cantered through a ravine along an overgrown path thick with blood-red, fleshy-looking flowers that looked as if their petals might open up and swallow them.

Insects whined around their heads; Storm flicked his ears irritably while Tom and Elenna slapped at their exposed skin. The foliage on either side almost closed over their heads, blotting out the sky. Wearily they climbed out of the deep green gloom and back on to higher ground. The jungle was close now.

As more lightning forked into the trees ahead, Silver stopped dead. He growled deep in his throat.

Elenna's hand went to her crossbow. "What is it, boy?"

Storm snorted in alarm and reared as the sky exploded. Hundreds of birds of all colours and sizes flew towards them in a shrieking mass.

The air was loud with the sound of beating wings.

"What is happening?" Elenna shouted.

Tom struggled to keep control of Storm, ducking in the saddle as the birds swooped over the top of his head. "I think they're fleeing something!" he yelled back.

The thrum in the air was deafening. As the birds arced away in formation, the ground started to rumble. A cloud of dust gathered at the mouth of the jungle. Silver howled. Storm wrenched his head back and forth as Tom clung to the reins.

"Animals!" Elenna shouted. "Hundreds of them!"

Monkeys screamed, tumbling through the dust ahead. Pumas, warthogs, orang-utans. Hundreds of

animals racing, roaring, snorting, bellowing and growling out of the trees as they headed straight towards Tom, Storm, Elenna and Silver.

"The creatures of the Misty Jungle are stampeding!" Tom gasped. "If we stay here, we'll be crushed!"

CHAPTER FOUR

DEATH IN THE JUNGLE

Tom yanked on Storm's reins, turning the stallion so hard that Storm almost lost his footing and Elenna half-slipped from the saddle behind him.

"We'll go back to the ravine!" he yelled at Elenna over his shoulder.

Silver ran ahead as Storm stretched out his neck and galloped back the way they had come. Elenna held on tightly as Tom wrapped his sweating hands around Storm's slippery reins. Choking dust was everywhere. Grit stung Tom's eyes.

"They're getting closer," Elenna cried.

Tom drove his heels into Storm's sides. The stallion found fresh strength and surged forward.

The path dropped so suddenly into the ravine that Tom and Elenna almost flew over Storm's head. Storm's hooves slipped as he scrabbled for grip.

"Get off the path," Elenna shouted. "We need to find cover!"

Tom steered Storm into the undergrowth, with Silver close at the stallion's heels. The noise behind grew like a marching army.

A heartbeat later, the animals charged past them. Tom and Elenna

peered, dumbstruck, through the bushes. The ravine walls boomed with the sound of the animals' cries and howls. Antelopes streaked down the ravine path, close to their hiding place. Tigers leaped overhead, their white bellies flashing briefly in the air before they reached the far side of the ravine.

When at last the air was still again,

Elenna drew a ragged breath. "What kind of Beast can scare a whole jungle?" she asked.

Tom was determined not to give in to the fear growing in his heart. "It's time we found out," he said.

They made their way back out of the ravine, to the edge of the jungle, oddly quiet since all its inhabitants had fled. The strange lightning had stopped, but the great black rip in the sky pulsed and shook, its edges obscured by the smoke rising from the burnt jungle plants.

"The trees here are too low to ride underneath," he said. "We'll walk."

As Tom dismounted and looped Storm's reins over his arm, Elenna slid down from the saddle and gripped her crossbow.

"I don't like this silence," she said,

gazing around. "It's so – unnatural."

Tom had been in several jungles during his Quests, but this was the eeriest. All he could hear was the snapping of twigs and the rustle of leaves beneath their feet. With one hand, Tom touched the magical yellow jewel in his belt that gave him a perfect memory. The shapes and paths of the Misty Jungle set in his mind like stone. *At least we won't get lost now,* he thought, drawing his heavy iron sword from its sheath.

The light filtering through the trees grew dim. Occasional rays of sunlight pierced the path where the trees lay broken, their foliage burnt away. Elenna coughed and drew her sleeve across her mouth. The smoke grew dense, swirling around their bodies. Storm whinnied uncertainly.

There was no sign of the Beast. Tom felt as defenceless as a fly, waiting for a great unseen hand to swoop down and swat him.

"If only we knew what kind of creature Ellik was," Elenna said. "Then I would feel more prepared. I wish it would show itself."

"It will," Tom said, glancing around. "We have to be patient."

Silver suddenly hurried on ahead into a burnt clearing. But he stopped suddenly, and howled. "He's found something," said Elenna. She ran over to him and gave a cry of dismay.

Tom joined her. A tangled heap of charred monkey corpses lay at his feet. He felt a surge of anger.

"I shouldn't have let us get caught by the soldiers," he muttered. "If I'd been quicker, we could have reached

this place before..." He pointed wordlessly at the innocent fallen creatures.

"It's not your fault, Tom," Elenna said. "It's Malvel's. Remember that."

Tom nodded, and tightened his grip on his sword. "While there's blood in my veins, I won't rest until Malvel is finished," he vowed. "However long it takes."

CHAPTER FIVE

FIRST SIGHT

Tom used his sword to hack into the undergrowth, slicing through sticky vines that dangled in front of them and roots that tangled around Storm's hooves. A sweet scent hung in the humid air. Sometimes they moved freely down paths cleared by the lightning, but before long they were caught in the thick mesh of leaves and branches once again.

Everything was as still and quiet as a graveyard.

Emerging from a dense path of jungle, Tom felt his foot sink into soft ground. "Stop," he said to the others, holding up his hand.

They gazed at the stretch of murky water in front of them.

"It's a swamp!" Elenna said.

The swamp was wide, spanning from left to right as far as Tom could see. Mangrove trees grew around the edges, their roots twisting up through the water like snakes. Tom could make out small islands dotted across the swamp's slick green surface, far away to the left. The opposite bank wasn't far, shifting in the mist which danced on the surface of the oily water.

"How are we going to get over it?"

Elenna asked with concern.

Tom took in the tangled undergrowth on either side, the trees packed together with hardly any space among the trunks. "We'll go across," he said.

"What about Storm and Silver?" Elenna said.

"They'll have to stay here," Tom said reluctantly, as Storm snorted and butted his head against Tom's shoulder.

Elenna looked uneasy. "But what about the Beast..."

"There's nothing else we can do," Tom said. "It's safer than trying to take them with us."

He picked up a thick branch that lay broken across the path, and held it upright in the water. "It's only waist deep," he said.

"But we should tie ourselves together, in case one of us gets into trouble."

He hacked at a vine that dangled from a nearby tree and lashed one end around his waist, while Elenna did the same with the other end.

Storm and Silver paced at the edge of the water as Tom and Elenna gingerly lowered themselves into the dank swamp. It lapped at Tom's waist, stinking and slimy, and seeped through his clothes. The mud sucked at his feet as he took a cautious step further out.

He looked back to see Elenna struggling behind him – and beyond her, Storm and Silver watching anxiously from the shore.

The only sound was the swamp rippling around them as they moved.

Tom's senses tingled.

There is danger here, he thought. Somewhere...

The mist thinned as they approached the opposite shore. Tom heard something. He stopped so abruptly that Elenna knocked into him, almost knocking him over.

"What was that?" he said.

"I didn't hear anything," Elenna replied with a frown.

Tom listened. There it was again. The cracking sound of twigs from the approaching bank. With no animals left, it could only mean one thing.

The Beast was waiting for them.

A patch of mist broke apart and Tom glimpsed a strange, blue glow among the trees. He saw rainbow-coloured fins flickering on a long body that slid along the ground, curling and knotting around the mangrove roots.

"Look," he whispered to Elenna. "Ellik is here."

The Beast's body seemed never-ending. She rippled along like a giant snake, fluid as water. Tom marvelled at the colours that danced on the creature's skin.

She was beautiful and terrifying at the same time.

"Has she seen us?" Elenna whispered, with her eyes fixed on the Beast.

Ellik raised her great scaly head and stared across the water. Her eyes were bright blue and sparking with coils of lightning.

She began moving swiftly towards the water's edge, her head poised to strike, her mouth open and her wicked fangs gleaming.

"I think the answer to that is yes," said Tom. He unsheathed his sword and lifted it, dripping, towards the bank. "Get out of the water, Elenna. Quickly!"

"No – our best defence is to stay here," insisted Elenna. She pulled a bolt from her quiver and tried to set it into her crossbow. "What can it do? It's on the bank and we're in here."

Ellik lunged into the water, fangs first. The water hissed and boiled.

To Tom's horror, he saw a sheet of blue light spreading beneath the surface towards him. Suddenly, his whole body juddered and white pain spread across his chest.

Dimly, Tom heard Elenna scream. He tried to move out of the water,

but his limbs weren't responding. Beneath him, his knees buckled and gave way.

Tom slid helplessly down into the swamp. The water closed over his head, filling his mouth and nostrils. He was completely powerless.

CHAPTER SIX

STORM TO THE RESCUE

Tom's lungs felt like they were going to burst. He saw Elenna in the water nearby. His friend was sinking, but he couldn't reach her.

We're going to drown, Tom thought in despair, *and I can't do anything about it.*

He could hardly blink, let alone move the arm that still clutched his sword. Where was Ellik?

Was she coming for them through the water at this very moment, her great long body gliding through the murk and her jaws open wide, preparing to rip and tear at their flesh?

Tom felt the vine around his waist tighten and realised that he was moving. Something was tugging him back through the swamp!

He managed to turn himself so that his face broke the surface, and choked up water with hacking coughs. Feeling returned to his limbs as he gasped and spluttered for breath. The moist swamp air tasted like nectar.

Tom heard Silver barking. Panic flooded him as he saw Elenna lying still, face down. Storm stood on the bank, his legs straining as he gripped

the end of the vine firmly between his teeth. The stallion had dug his hooves into the ground. Mud splattered up his long black legs as he pulled Tom and Elenna free of the water. Weakly, Tom managed to roll Elenna over and heaved her onto the bank. He scrabbled ashore beside her.

To his relief, she began to cough, her face creased in pain. Water frothed out over her chin, but she managed a smile.

"Are you all right?" Tom asked, cradling his friend.

She nodded, as Silver came forward to lick her wet face.

Storm dropped the end of the vine, and whickered at Tom.

"Thank you," he said in wonder, reaching out to stroke the stallion's velvet nose. "You saved us, Storm!"

The tips of Tom's fingers and toes still tingled, but the pain had lessened in most of his body now. Only his hand still hurt. Tom looked at his palm, and saw that an outline of the hilt of his sword had been burnt into the skin like a cattle brand. The wound was blistered and raw.

Rubbing water from his eyes, Tom looked around for his sword and saw it resting, hilt up, in some dense weeds not far from the bank. He leaned over and plucked it out with his good hand.

"What kind of Beast has power like that?" said Elenna, climbing gingerly to her feet.

"That wasn't strength, or cunning, or any of the things we've faced in former Beasts," Tom said grimly. "It was like being hit by lightning! How are we ever going to fight against such a weapon?"

There was no sign of the Beast. The water was calm and the jungle was quieter than ever.

"I don't think Ellik's in the water anymore," said Elenna, scanning the swamp. "We'd see a trail of bubbles, or ripples. She must have gone over to the other side again."

Waiting for us, Tom thought.

"We can't risk wading across again," he said. "Next time, we may not be so lucky. We'll have to find a way round."

They set off wearily along the bank of the swamp, their clothes sodden with foul-smelling water. The jungle trees pressed in on either side of them. Light glimmered faintly through their tangled roots and branches.

Tom tried to ignore the pain piercing his blistered hand, and instead concentrated on helping Storm lift his hooves through the roots. Silver hopped between them, agile as ever.

"Look," cried Elenna, pointing

through the trees ahead of them at a scattering of rocks stretching across the swamp. "Do you think we can use them as stepping stones?"

"It's worth a try," said Tom, as he looped Storm's reins around a branch. "Sorry, boy. We need you to wait here."

"Look after each other," said Elenna to Silver. The wolf lay down beside Storm, his head on his paws.

Tom led the way, stepping carefully on the rocks, with Elenna close behind him. The stones were slimy with thick green moss.

All the while, Tom scanned the swamp, his sword in his hand. Hundreds of fish lay belly up in the water, their silver scales glinting in the weak light that filtered through the jungle mist.

The shock that had nearly killed Tom and Elenna had been too much for them.

Tom leapt from the final stepping stone into the soft mud of the opposite bank. Elenna jumped after him, catching onto a branch to steady herself. Glimmering in the trees in front of them hung a strange, transparent sheet of material.

It swayed in the humid air as Tom prodded it with the tip of his sword.

"Urgh," said Elenna with a shudder. "What is it?"

The pale green jungle light brought out a diamond pattern on the material. And Tom realised what it was.

"It's Ellik's skin," he said. "She must have shed it, the way a snake does."

Elenna stared at the enormous expanse of skin. It stretched away into the trees. "Snakes shed their skin when they grow," she said. "Just how big is this creature?"

Tom sliced through the snakeskin, pushing it aside like a hideous curtain. "It's time to find out," he said, and plunged into the darkness on the other side.

CHAPTER SEVEN

HIDE AND SEEK

As Tom and his friend pressed deeper into the Misty Jungle, the destruction caused by the lightning became worse. There were broken, charred skeletons of trees everywhere Tom looked. Undergrowth was burned away to bare rock, which still smoked and smouldered red against the barren ground.

There were more animal carcasses

too, scattered on the ground where the poor creatures had met their ends. No wonder all the other creatures were in such a rush to escape, Tom thought.

The anger that ran through him gave him new strength. They would defeat this Beast, or die in the attempt.

But there was still no sign of the Lightning Horror. Tom was confused. Was she hiding? For a creature with powers as awesome as Ellik, it made no sense. Perhaps she was lying in wait for them with her dripping fangs.

They struggled out of the trees and into a clearing. Tom wiped the sweat from his eyes. A rocky outcrop loomed before them. The stones were grey and glistening with moisture, lush ferns growing among the damp nooks and crannies.

“Where is she?” Elenna whispered.

Tom gazed around. In the rock face he made out the dark mouths of ten or twelve caves. They had wide, jagged entrances large enough to drive a cart through. Certainly big enough for a Beast.

“She may be hiding in one of these caves,” Tom said to Elenna, moving towards the largest opening in the rocks. “You check the ones over there. Call me if you find anything.”

The first cave burst to life as soon as Tom set foot inside. A family of tiny mice fled for the light, darting between Tom’s feet and making him jump. When his heart stopped hammering, Tom allowed himself a smile. Ellik hadn’t driven all of the jungle inhabitants away after all.

But inside, the cave was far too

small for a Beast to lurk. He moved to the next. The pain made him wince. Tom knew his injured hand gave Ellik another advantage. He swapped his sword to his left hand, testing himself by swinging it around in circles. It wasn't perfect, but it would have to do. He had fought this way before, when Krabb had poisoned his sword hand in Gwildor.

"Nothing in those caves," Elenna said, running over to join Tom. "Have you tried that one yet?"

They entered the cavemouth side by side, descending a little before emerging into a huge cavern. Its roof stood as tall as three or four storeys. It felt as if they were in the mouth of some hideous giant. The stalagmites on the ground and the stalactites dripping from the ceiling looked like teeth waiting to close on them.

The cave was the right size for Ellik, but as Tom made his way among the maze of stalagmites – some almost touching the stalactites stretching downwards – he could see that the Beast wasn't there. The rest of the caves were empty as well. As they emerged from the last cave – a narrow cleft that Tom had barely been able to squeeze his body through – Elenna sat down on the ground.

"It's like a game of hide and seek," she said angrily.

The air outside the caves had thickened. Rain began to fall, spattering through the mist onto Tom's face and neck. He could make out dark storm clouds rolling in the sky. The portal pulsed, grey and distant overhead.

"Should we take shelter back in the cave?" Elenna asked.

"Finding the Beast is more important," Tom decided. "We need to go back among the trees."

The rain fell harder. It should have been refreshing, but the jungle heat made it warm and unpleasant. At least it washed the stench of the swamp water from their clothes.

As they passed a stand of trees that stretched their foliage high up into the misty canopy, Tom felt something like a shiver pass over his arms. He looked down and saw the hairs on his arms standing on end.

"Tom, your hair!" Elenna gasped. "It's sticking straight up!"

"Yours too," Tom said. Elenna's hair was bristling as if blown by the wind. But the air was still. Tom's pulse quickened. "Ellik is nearby," he muttered. "The energy is coming from her, Elenna. I'm sure of it."

Tom's breath caught in his throat as he saw a blue glow between the plants ahead. Ellik had coiled her gleaming body around the trunk of a nearby tree, and was watching them with her fierce eyes. Her tongue darted out, tasting the air. Her chilling hiss was like the rustle of leaves.

Water dripped from above. It sizzled as it landed on the Beast, throwing off clouds of steam that billowed and blended with the mist. Lightning forked overhead, splitting the sky.

Tom had an idea. "We'll draw her out," he said. "If we can get her away from the cover of the trees, perhaps the lightning will strike her."

Elenna and Tom moved away from

the trees, back to the rocky outcrop with its clear stretch of sky. Elenna kept her crossbow trained at the creature's head and Tom held his sword in his left hand.

Ellik blinked slowly, then uncoiled herself from the tree and slid into the clearing. She opened a rainbow-coloured hood of skin that fanned out on either side of her head. Overhead, the storm clouds rumbled. Tom realised that the lightning had as much chance of striking him or Elenna as it did of hitting the Beast.

There was a flash in the sky. A white hot blade of lightning tore through the mist and caught Ellik squarely on the back of her neck.

"We got her!" Elenna shouted.

But the Beast seemed only to glow more brightly than before. Her eyes flared like the embers of a fire as she reared up, ready to strike.

"No!" Tom gasped as he realised their mistake. "The lightning doesn't harm her – it makes her stronger!"

CHAPTER EIGHT

DEADLY ENERGY

Everything fell into place in one terrible moment. The weird lightning flickering over the Misty Jungle... The bolt of energy in the water... And now the Beast, fully charged and more dangerous than ever.

Tom pulled his shield off his back and held it between himself and Ellik, peering over the rim. The Beast's rainbow-coloured fins waved and her immense body pulsed with power from the sky. Tom was rooted to the spot as Ellik opened her terrible mouth and let out a hissing breath. Arching back her head to reveal her long fangs, the Beast struck, spitting out a bolt of lightning that flew towards them like white hot death.

Tom ducked behind his shield. The force of the bolt crashed into the wood, knocking Tom backwards and

rattling his bones. The air around him was blinding white. His shield felt hot, smoke rising from its battle-scarred surface. Tom risked a glance over his shoulder.

"Elenna!" he shouted, unable to see her through the smoke. "Are you hurt?"

"Don't worry about me!" Elenna called.

Tom's vision returned. He saw Elenna jump up onto the glistening rocks and fitted a bolt into her crossbow. She fired the shaft and it lodged into the Beast's thick scales. Ellik hissed angrily, but kept her eyes fixed on Tom.

"I'll lure her into the trees!" Tom called to Elenna, backing away.

The air rippled as Ellik fired another stream of lighting. Tom ducked.

A nearby bush burst into flame. He turned and ran for the trees. Branches exploded overhead as the Lightning Horror pursued him, shooting bolt after bolt. Each one seemed less powerful than the one before, but Tom couldn't be sure. Tom brought his shield up, deflecting the cascade of burning debris.

He twisted through the trees, dodging Ellik's attacks, which were definitely growing weaker. He risked a glance over his shoulder. The Beast was struggling, pulling her long body through the tangle of trees as she pursued him. She didn't belong in this jungle. Tom realised that each blast of power was using up her reserves and slowing her down.

He felt a surge of fresh hope. *She has a weakness after all,* he thought.

He almost fell as the trees thinned abruptly and he found himself in another clearing. Ellik slithered after him, crashing into trees and bushes, flattening them under her bulk. Hatred seethed in her eyes.

She reared to fire another bolt, but all that emerged from her fangs was a plume of smoke. The blue glow had left her body, and now her scales were black and dull.

She lay slumped in the clearing, breathing hard. Tom moved towards her, his sword poised. He'd learnt on his previous Quests that he didn't have to kill Tavania's Beasts. To bring them under control and send them home, he had to have them at his mercy.

"Elenna, she's run out of power!" he shouted. "She's harmless now. Come and..."

Lightning flashed. The light made Tom throw his shield up to protect his eyes. His chest tightened. *Please no,* he thought. But when he lowered his arm he saw that the lightning had struck Ellik. She was glowing fiercely again, her body crackling with power.

She reared up. Her eyes flashed as she spread her hood. Tom flung himself to one side as a spear of white light seared the air. The tree behind him became a pile of ash.

I have to get Ellik somewhere the lightning can't strike her, he thought.

But where?

As the Beast hissed and prepared to send down another deadly bolt of lightning, Tom dodged back past her the way he'd come. A huge tree burst into flame beside him as he ran, bathing him in baking heat.

He flung himself at a low branch and scrambled upwards, trying to ignore the screaming pain in his hand as the bark rubbed against his raw flesh. If he could just climb high enough...

Trees burned below him, and thick smoke spiralled upwards. Tom clambered on, reaching from branch to branch.

When he looked down, he saw Ellik slithering across the jungle floor below. He was safe for a moment – the Beast hadn't seen him.

The glow of Ellik's body had faded once again. Tom watched from his perch high in the tree as she flickered her tongue, tasting the air in search of her prey. As quietly as he could, Tom climbed along the branch and

hopped into the next tree, keeping Ellik in his sights. Through the branches, he could see Elenna still standing on the rocks where he had left her. He waved his arm to attract her attention. When he was sure she could see him, he batted the air with his hand to indicate that Ellik was coming back. She had to hide!

Elenna pointed beneath her,

at the rocks where she was standing. She was mouthing something. Tom strained his eyes to read her lips. It looked like she was saying "Caves".

In a flash, Tom realised Elenna had found the answer. If he could persuade Ellik into the big cave they'd explored earlier, the lightning wouldn't be able to penetrate the rock. But how could he get there without Ellik turning him to ashes?

There was a cracking sound, and Tom swayed on the branch. Startled, he looked down. He was too far from the trunk of the tree! The branch beneath his feet was splintering and about to give way.

With a cry of desperation, he flung himself towards the tree trunk as the branch shattered and fell to the jungle floor. He gripped the trunk, catching his breath, and looked down.

Ellik's eyes were locked on him and fury burned in the glassy orbs. Another fork of lightning blazed down from the sky, filling her with terrifying power. She wrapped her body around the trunk of the tree and began to climb. There was nowhere he could run.

CHAPTER NINE

DEFEAT

Ellik moved quickly, her muscular body pushing itself up the trunk.

There's no escape, Tom thought.

Ellik opened her jaws and sent out a jet of pure light. Faced with no other option, Tom pushed off the trunk and leapt into the air. The top of the tree exploded in a burst of flame.

Tom's hands grasped frantically at

the air – and he felt a vine. Pain scorched his injured palm, but Tom held on, swinging wildly back and forth on a vine. His sword slipped from its sheath and tumbled through the branches towards the ground. There was no time to think about that now. Ellik dropped down from the tree and slithered after him, darting her fangs to snatch him from the air.

Using his legs, Tom thrust himself aside, letting go of the vine and seizing on another mid-air. He grabbed it, swinging again as more lightning poured from the boiling sky and into Ellik. She slithered across the ground beneath him, looking for an opportunity to strike.

Tom swung from vine to vine like a monkey, back towards the caves.

His shoulders and arms screamed with pain, but he knew if he let go now, he'd fall to the jungle floor and probably break his neck. Ellik was freeing herself from a tangle of roots below, as he let go of the last vine and crashed to the ground, rolling over and over. His shield was gone, too. He was back in the clearing, lying at the foot of the rocky outcrop. But Elenna was no longer there.

There was no time to look for her. Tom struggled to his feet dizzily. The cave wasn't far. But Ellik was moving out of the trees. She reared, sparks gathering between her fangs.

Tom's legs weren't moving as fast as he wanted them to.

This is it, he thought. *I'm doomed.*

Ellik fired. The air blazed. And suddenly Elenna was there, clutching Tom's shield. She hurled herself across Tom's body and held it up to protect them both. Tom's ears sang as the bolt struck the shield at full force.

"This way!" Elenna grabbed Tom's sleeve and tugged him behind a scattering of rocks.

"We have to get Ellik into that cave where the lightning can't hit her," Tom gasped.

He and Elenna peered around the

rocks. The mouth of the cave was twenty paces away, across a patch of exposed ground.

"She'll see us if we run for it," said Elenna.

"We want her to see us," Tom said. "We just need a head start."

Tom could see the Beast's great head swinging back and forth, searching for them among the caves. Tom cast his eyes around for something to distract her. They only needed a little time. His fingers closed on a small rock. He flung it hard at the Beast's tail.

Ellik hissed and turned her head, firing a lightning bolt behind her. Seizing their chance, Tom and Elenna sprinted for the cave.

Ellik rounded on them, and a fresh bolt of fire hit the ground by their feet as they flung themselves into the darkness.

"She'll follow us in," Tom said, wiping his forehead. He felt defenceless without his sword, but knew he still had to fight the Beast somehow. "We have to go in as deep as we can."

Dim light filtered into the cave mouth. Suddenly, Ellik's head filled the entrance. A bolt of lightning tore into the base of a stalagmite near Tom. With a booming sound that echoed through the cavern, it collapsed beside him.

Tom leaped onto a ledge on the cave wall and ran deeper into the darkness. He'd lost sight of Elenna.

Ellik paused for moment at the entrance, then slithered into the cave, her coils twisting between the dank columns of stalagmites as she tried to find Tom. More bolts of lightning smashed around the cave, flashing bright against the rough walls and throwing shadows across the cave. Tom pressed himself close to the cave wall as stalactites rained down, their murderous points

shattering on impact with the ground.

The back of the cave loomed. Tom skidded to a halt, almost losing his balance on the ledge. The cave wasn't as deep as he'd thought. He looked around quickly and saw Elenna on the far side of the cave, fitting a bolt to her crossbow. There was another ledge higher up the back wall of the cave. If he could reach it...

Ellik made up the distance to Tom quickly, and reared in front of him, less than ten paces away. The light from the cave mouth threw her into terrible silhouette as she flared her hood. Tom's back was pressed up to the cave wall, but there was nowhere he could go. The Beast opened her mouth and Tom threw himself to the ground as, above him, a burst of lightning struck the cave wall, where his head had been, showering jagged rock and dust down on Tom's face.

Tom started scrabbling away, when he became aware of something...

Ellik no longer grunted and growled with furious intent, but with angry frustration. Tom dared to look back at the Beast, and saw her struggling to release her coils from the stalagmites she had twined herself through, hissing hopelessly.

"Her power's drained," shouted Elenna. "Now's our chance!"

Tom leaped down from the ledge and beside the broken point of a fallen stalagmite. It was slick with moisture and heavy, like lifting an anvil in the blacksmith's.

He struggled to lift it above his head, and staggered until he was standing over Ellik's prone body. The Beast squirmed and hissed with anger. At last, the Lightning Horror of the Misty Jungle was at his mercy.

"This is the end," he shouted,

gazing down into Ellik's eyes. "It's time to send you home."

Ellik's head sank down onto the cave floor, and her eyes dimmed. She knew she was defeated. Tom lowered the stalagmite and let it fall to the ground.

Though the Beast had nearly killed him, Tom knew it was only because she was lost and frightened, ripped from her natural habitat and cast into this place by Malvel's evil. Now she was going home.

The rocky walls began to rumble, and the whole cavern seemed to shake beneath Tom's feet. Cracks appeared in the stones above them, and dust and pebbles showered down.

"Get out, Tom!" Elenna screamed. "The roof is caving in!"

CHAPTER TEN

REUNITED

Tom struggled to stay on his feet as he stared wide-eyed at the gap opening up in the cave roof. But something strange was happening. The cave hadn't collapsed on top of them.

Tom darted to Elenna, near the entrance. "It's all right," he said. He laughed in amazement. "Look! The rocks are falling *up*!"

It was the most extraordinary thing

he'd ever seen. Instead of crashing into the cave, the broken fragments of the roof blew outwards, spiralling into the sky. A huge slab of rock broke away and flew upwards, revealing the great portal throbbing and crackling in the molten sky. Boulders the size of barrels spun through the air.

Tom moved back, pulling Elenna with him. They flattened themselves against the cave wall and watched as broken stalactites and stalagmites rose from the rocky ground, teetered on their points and flying upwards.

"It's incredible!" Elenna gasped.

Ellik was the last to move. Her great body unwound from the stalagmites like a blue-black ribbon. Her transparent fins shone brightly as the light poured through them,

scattering rainbows across the cave.

She rose up through the hole in the roof and into the bright air, growing smaller until she was almost a dot in the centre of the portal. Then she vanished, and the torn edges of the portal closed around her, sealing and shrinking to nothing. With a flash, the sky was whole again.

In the still air of the cave, loose stones skittered across the ground.

"Ellik has really gone," Elenna said in wonder. "You did it!"

"We did it," said Tom. "If it hadn't been for your plan to lure her into the cave, we'd both be dead."

Together they walked wearily out of the cave. Tom picked up his shield from where it lay battered and singed on the rocky ground outside the cave. Elenna found his sword embedded point down in the base of a tree.

Tom remembered the way back as clearly as if it had been etched onto his mind. He touched the yellow jewel at his belt by way of thanks, and led Elenna through the tangled thickets, across clearings and around rocky outcrops – until they found themselves at the stepping stones and the swamp once again.

Silver started barking the moment Tom and Elenna stepped onto the first stone. Storm whinnied, rearing up and thrashing the air with his hooves.

"Enough!" Elenna laughed as she reached the other side. She stroked Silver's grey head as the wolf licked her face and leaned his paws on her shoulders. Tom patted Storm on the neck as the stallion butted his nose into his chest and whickered at him with delight.Above, a bird cried out, and Tom saw a green parrot alight on a nearby branch.

"It looks like the animals know it's safe to return," he said.

A small deer bounded into view through the trees.

"Soon the forest will return to normal," said Elenna, smiling.

Tom drew a breath as something flew low over their heads. It was a falcon. The bird tipped its blue-grey wings and landed on one of the mossy stepping stones. It clicked its sharp beak and cocked its head.

"Isn't that Oradu's bird?" said Elenna.

Before Tom could answer, a voice said, "It is indeed!" Tom and his friend turned as one to see a shimmering vision of Oradu standing among the trees. The Good Wizard of Tavania looked more complete than ever, dressed in his robe and hat with his staff in his hand. His face still remained ghostly, but he was smiling.

"Congratulations, all of you," Oradu said in his deep voice. "Ellik has gone home, and by your valiant efforts, you have returned this to me." From inside his cloak, he brought out a small iron cauldron.

With each Quest they completed, the Good Wizard's powers returned. Soon he would be complete, and ready to face Malvel again.

"How is my mother?" Tom asked. "And Dalaton? Has she finished training him to be a hero? Are they still at Malvel's castle?"

"Freya and Dalaton are doing well," Oradu replied. "They are preparing for the battle with Malvel that will surely come. They have friends, too."

He passed his hand over the top of the cauldron. It sparked and simmered, throwing up a ghostly image of Freya and Dalaton. Tom couldn't believe the change in the former prison guard. The pasty, overweight man he had first met when they came to Tavania had all but disappeared. In his place was a strong, confident man who was starting to look more and more like a warrior.

The cauldron trembled in Oradu's hands. "I grow weak," said the wizard, lowering the cauldron regretfully. "You have triumphed up till now, but the final Beast..."

He shimmered and vanished, his words fading with him. His robes and cauldron magically shrank and then tucked themselves away in Storm's saddlebags. The falcon flew away.

"One more Beast," said Elenna. "Then Tavania will be safe."

"Not quite," said Tom grimly. "Tavania will never be safe while Malvel sits on the throne."

"We've defeated him before," said Elenna. "We can do it again."

Tom looked at his brave friend, with Silver and Storm at her side.

With companions like these, he knew he wouldn't fail.

Here's a sneak preview of Tom's next exciting adventure!

Meet

CarnivorA THE WINGED SCAVENGER

Only Tom can save Tavania from the rule of the Evil Wizard Malvel...

PROLOGUE

Tobias narrowed his eyes against the icy wind as he trudged across the Frozen Fields of Tavania towards his ice lodging. Behind him, he dragged the sack of fish he'd just caught. The rope cut into his hands, even through his thick leather mittens.

It was a good catch, he thought. *If I can sell all the fish in the market, I'll have enough money to last me through this dreadful season.*

Pausing to rest, Tobias looked up at the domed sky of Tavania. He was sure it was hanging lower than it once did. Worse than that, a dark rip stretched across it, from above his head almost to the horizon. Its edges looked like tattered shreds of cloud, and beyond them was a menacing dark portal. Tobias couldn't imagine where it might lead.

"It gives me the creeps," he muttered. "And I'm not the only one."

Last time he had visited the market, all talk had been of the dreadful split in the sky.

"Is this the end of Tavania?" people were asking each other.

Tobias shook his head. There's no point in upsetting myself, he thought. He knew that Tavania had seen hard times before, and no doubt there would be hard times again. But his people had always been survivors.

A yap sounded from across the icefield as Karwai, Tobias's pet Arctic fox, bounded towards him.

Follow this Quest to the end in CARNIVORA THE WINGED SCAVENGER.

Win an exclusive Beast Quest T-shirt and goody bag!

Tom has battled many fearsome Beasts and we want to know which one is your favourite! Send us a drawing or painting of your favourite Beast and tell us in 30 words why you think it's the best.

Each month we will select **three** winners to receive a Beast Quest T-shirt and goody bag!

Send your entry on a postcard to
BEAST QUEST COMPETITION
Orchard Books, 338 Euston Road, London NW1 3BH.

Australian readers should email:
childrens.books@hachette.com.au

New Zealand readers should write to:
Beast Quest Competition, 4 Whetu Place, Mairangi Bay, Auckland NZ, or email: childrensbooks@hachette.co.nz

Don't forget to include your name and address.
Only one entry per child.

Good luck!

Beast Quest®

1. Ferno the Fire Dragon
2. Sepron the Sea Serpent
3. Arcta the Mountain Giant
4. Tagus the Horse-Man
5. Nanook the Snow Monster
6. Epos the Flame Bird

Beast Quest:
The Golden Armour

7. Zepha the Monster Squid
8. Claw the Giant Monkey
9. Soltra the Stone Charmer
10. Vipero the Snake Man
11. Arachnid the King of Spiders
12. Trillion the Three-Headed Lion

Beast Quest:
The Dark Realm

13. Torgor the Minotaur
14. Skor the Winged Stallion
15. Narga the Sea Monster
16. Kaymon the Gorgon Hound
17. Tusk the Mighty Mammoth
18. Sting the Scorpion Man

Beast Quest:
The Amulet of Avantia

19. Nixa the Death Bringer
20. Equinus the Spirit Horse
21. Rashouk the Cave Troll
22. Luna the Moon Wolf
23. Blaze the Ice Dragon
24. Stealth the Ghost Panther

Beast Quest:
The Shade of Death

25. Krabb Master of the Sea
26. Hawkite Arrow of the Air
27. Rokk the Walking Mountain
28. Koldo the Arctic Warrior
29. Trema the Earth Lord
30. Amictus the Bug Queen

Beast Quest:
The World of Chaos

31. Komodo the Lizard King
32. Muro the Rat Monster
33. Fang the Bat Fiend
34. Murk the Swamp Man
35. Terra Curse of the Forest
36. Vespick the Wasp Queen

Beast Quest:
The Lost World

37. Convol the Cold-Blooded Brute
38. Hellion the Fiery Foe
39. Krestor the Crushing Terror
40. Madara the Midnight Warrior
41. Ellik the Lightning Horror
42. Carnivora the Winged Scavenger

Beast Quest:
The Pirate King

43. Balisk the Water Snake
44. Koron Jaws of Death
45. Hecton the Body Snatcher
46. Torno the Hurricane Dragon
47. Kronus the Clawed Menace
48. Bloodboar the Buried Doom

Beast Quest:
The Warlock's Staff

49. Ursus the Clawed Roar
50. Minos the Demon Bull
51. Koraka the Winged Assassin
52. Silver the Wild Terror
53. Spikefin the Water King
54. Torpix the Twisting Serpent

Beast Quest:
Master of the Beasts

55. Noctila the Death Owl
56. Shamani the Raging Flame
57. Lustor the Acid Dart
58. Voltrex the Two-Headed Octopus
59. Tecton the Armoured Giant
60. Doomskull the King of Fear

Beast Quest:
The New Age

61. Elko Lord of the Sea
62. Tarrok the Blood Spike
63. Brutus the Hound of Horror
64. Flaymar the Scorched Blaze
65. Serpio the Slithering Shadow
66. Tauron the Pounding Fury

Beast Quest:
The Darkest Hour

67. Solak Scourge of the Sea
68. Kajin the Beast Catcher
69. Issrilla the Creeping Menace
70. Vigrash the Clawed Eagle
71. Mirka the Ice Horse
72. Kama the Faceless Beast

Special Bumper Editions

Vedra & Krimon: Twin Beasts of Avantia
Spiros the Ghost Phoenix
Arax the Soul Stealer
Kragos & Kildor: The Two-Headed Demon
Creta the Winged Terror
Mortaxe the Skeleton Warrior
Ravira, Ruler of the Underworld
Raksha the Mirror Demon
Grashkor the Beast Guard
Ferrok the Iron Soldier

All books priced at £4.99.
Special bumper editions priced at £5.99.

Orchard Books are available from all good bookshops, or can be ordered from our website: www.orchardbooks.co.uk, or telephone 01235 827702, or fax 01235 8227703.

Series 7: THE LOST WORLD
COLLECT THEM ALL!

Can Tom save the chaotic land of Tavania from dark Wizard Malvel's evil plans?

978 1 40830 729 8

978 1 40830 730 4

978 1 40830 731 1

978 1 40830 732 8

978 1 40830 733 5

978 1 40830 734 2

Series 8: THE PIRATE KING
OUT NOW!

Sanpao the Pirate King wants to steal the sacred Tree of Being. Can Tom scupper his plans?

978 1 40831 310 7

978 1 40831 311 4

978 1 40831 312 1

978 1 40831 313 8

978 1 40831 314 5

978 1 40831 315 2